Weekly Reader Books presents

THE
SNAILMAN

BRENDA SIVERS

Illustrated by Shirley Hughes

Boston   Little, Brown and Company   Toronto

This book is a presentation of Weekly Reader Books.
Weekly Reader Books offers book clubs for children from
preschool to young adulthood. All quality hardcover books are selected
by a distinguished Weekly Reader Selection Board.

For further information write to:
Weekly Reader Books
1250 Fairwood Ave.
Columbus, Ohio 43216

Library of Congress Cataloging in Publication Data

Sivers, Brenda.
    The snailman.

    SUMMARY: Recently moved to a country village, Timothy
is bored and lonely until he meets the eccentric snailman who is feared and avoided by the rest of the towns-
people.
    [1. Friendship — Fiction. 2. Country life — Fiction]
I. Hughes, Shirley. II. Title.
PZ7.S6237Sn   [Fic]   78-9297
ISBN 0-316-79118-0

Published simultaneously in Canada
by Little, Brown & Company (Canada) Limited

PRINTED IN THE UNITED STATES OF AMERICA

For Mark and Jeremy

Timothy Eden wandered aimlessly down the hill, kicking at stones and slashing the heads off dog roses with a stick. He was bored. He was lonely. In fact, he decided, hurling a pebble at a huge crow, he had never been unhappier in his life.

As the pebble flew by, the bird cawed angrily and flapped its wings at the boy. "Caw! Caw!" mimicked Timothy, sticking out his tongue and flapping imaginary wings in return. The crow rose from the ground, up, up into the sky and flew lazily away.

"Wish I could fly away," thought Timothy enviously. "I'd go straight back to our old home." And he swallowed hard at the memory of the little flat in South London where he and his parents had lived for as long as he could remember. London, he thought, with its crowded streets, its cinemas and shops, its noise and bustle. London with all his old friends, his aunts and uncles and Granny and Granpa . . . Leaving them behind, leaving them forever, just to live in this dreary little village, was more than he could bear.

If only he could fly away, if only . . .

Suddenly he heard voices and the next moment a blond head appeared over the brow of the hill, followed by a second and third. Every nerve in Timothy's body sounded the alarm and, without stopping to think, he leaped into the hedgerow, landing squarely in a patch of welcoming nettles.

5

It wasn't that he was afraid of the three Payne brothers, although he had good reason to be. More than once they had set upon him, lying in ambush as he came home from school and beating him until his nose ran red and his eyes were bruised. But more than fearing them, Timothy despised them. He knew their strength lay in numbers. Apart, they were cowardly, only too anxious to tell tales and curry favor, and, if he ever got the chance to tackle them separately, Timothy knew he would give them the thrashing of their lives . . . or, at least, he would have a good try.

But today they were together, prowling around the countryside looking for somebody to torment. And discretion, Timothy decided from the safety of the hedgerow, was in this case the better part of valor, although he wished he'd chosen a more comfortable place to hide. The nettles stung him unmercifully, pricking his skin with a thousand red-hot needles that made him wince with pain. But he dared not move, not even to scratch at the tiny white spots that were already covering his bare legs and arms.

As the brothers swaggered by, Timothy noticed that Harry, as usual, was in the lead. Harry wasn't the oldest of the Paynes but, at eleven, he was the strongest—thickset and muscular, his round moon face balancing on a bull neck. Frank came next. He was a tall, gangling boy who had grown too quickly and seemed embarrassed by his long legs and arms. Tom, the youngest, brought up the rear.

"Course 'e'll be there," Harry was saying to his brothers, as if to urge them on; " 'e's always there." And he stooped to pick up the stick that Timothy had dropped in his flight. "Come on!" he shouted, brandishing the stick like a sword. " 'E'll be playin' with 'is 'orrible snails."

And they all broke into a run.

Timothy quickly realized what mischief they were up to. It was the old game, one of their favorites. When they weren't bullying younger children or hurting small animals, they went up to Carpenters' Hill and baited Bob, the snailman.

Timothy didn't even know what Bob's real name was. The boy had lived in the village for almost four months and had never seen the man, but he had never heard anybody refer to him as anything but Bob, the snailman.

The man seemed to obsess the villagers. Almost from the day he arrived, Timothy heard about the strange man who lived on the hill, for, whenever a few people were gathered together for a chat, inevitably Bob, the snailman, would creep into their conversation.

They suspected him of a thousand unnatural acts, none of which they could prove, but the whispering and slandering never seemed to stop.

Timothy listened, intrigued, but his questions about the snailman were invariably met with a wag of the finger and an admonishment not to go near him.

"Why!" Timothy had asked.

"Because he's weird," came the answer. "Funny in the head. So would you be if you kept snails for pets."

"Snails!" Timothy echoed, fascinated yet repelled by the idea.

"Aye. They live in the house with him. Hundreds o' them."

At that point Timothy's informant would tap the side of his head. "Loony, if you ask me."

When the Paynes were a safe distance from him, Timothy disentangled himself from the hedgerow and scratched furiously at his legs, which were now covered with large white welts from the nettles.

Initially he had wanted to see the snailman, despite the warnings, and now his curiosity was aroused again. He had built a picture of the snailman in his mind. He imagined him to be some kind of a monster, a hideous cross between Frankenstein and the Hunchback of Notre Dame, and he wanted to see how the Payne brothers would approach such a fearful creature. And, since there was nothing better to do—there never was these days—he crept back up the hill, keeping close to bushes and trees lest the Paynes should turn and see him and make him the object of their sport.

They were standing in front of a three-bar gate, jeering and making grotesque faces at someone who was still out of Timothy's vision. As he drew nearer, he heard the boys chanting a rhyme that was already becoming very familiar to him:

"Bad old Bob. He's a slob.

No one wants to give him a job.

So he has to cadge and rob.

Bad old, sad old, mad old Bob!"

The chant was repeated monotonously, accompanied by vulgar noises and expressions to match. Timothy stealthily climbed a fence into a field opposite the snailman's property and, hiding behing a tree, he peeked around it. From his new vantage point he could see a small stone house about twenty feet from the gate. Bushes snuggled up against its walls, and vines grew haphazardly, threatening to cover the tiny casement windows and reach up to the moss-covered tiles on the roof. There were numerous outbuildings and sheds, all newly painted, and a large greenhouse in the far corner, which sheltered row upon row of lettuce and tomato plants. A cow and some goats and sheep grazed peacefully nearby, oblivious to the shouts and jeers of the boys in the lane.

The door of the house was open and Timothy could make out the figure of a man, his back toward them. He was hunched over, working intently at some kind of machine, his hands moving from side to side in a rhythmical manner. Inching closer, Timothy recognized the machine. It was a loom, just like the one he had seen at an arts and crafts exhibition in London. And now he could see the length of brightly colored plaid the man was weaving.

Timothy felt cheated. From everything he had heard, he had expected the snailman to be a raging maniac, frothing at the mouth and pulling babies limb from limb. Instead, here he was quietly weaving, throwing the shuttle back and forth in a smooth, regular motion, unaware—or uncaring—of the taunts and yells from the trio at the gate.

And there were no snails in sight. Not one. At least, not as far as Timothy could see from the other side of the lane.

A small notice nailed to the tree warned, "Private. Keep out," and Timothy observed that, despite their bravado, the Payne brothers heeded it.

Finally, however, frustrated by the man's quiet concentration, Harry picked up a heavy stone.

The youngest brother grabbed his arm. " 'Ere, watch it!" he cautioned. But Harry shook him off, and, raising his arm, took aim at the back of the man's head.

At that moment a furious yelping broke out and a large collie leaped from his resting place at the snailman's feet and hurled himself down the path at the gate. He flattened himself on the dusty ground and drew back his lips in a snarl. Keeping his eyes firmly on the Paynes, he edged toward them, ready to attack the slightest hostile movement. The Paynes shrank back, lanky Frank trying to hide behind Harry while Harry, the brave, pushed his youngest brother in the path of the growling dog.

Still keeping his back toward them, the snailman rose and stretched his arms, as if to relieve their stiffness. Timothy drew in his breath sharply. The man was huge. He stood poised, arms and legs stretched out like a huge crossbow, ready to aim its strength in any direction.

PRIVATE
KEEP OUT

Harry Payne suddenly had second thoughts about throwing the stone, and he dropped it limply on the road. "Come on," he muttered to his brothers, glancing furtively at the gigantic back and the still snarling dog, "It ain't no fun 'ere."

And the trio loped away.

When they had gone, the snailman sat down and started to weave again. The dog returned to his place, stretching out by his master's chair, and the cow and sheep continued their contented munching as if nothing untoward had happened. For a while Timothy stood and watched. And then a foolish idea came to him. A very foolish idea. Easing himself over the fence, he tiptoed across the lane and, one foot poised ready to run, he started to chant in a small, quavery voice:

"Bad old Bob. He's a slob.

No one wants to give him a job.

So he has to cadge . . ."

His voice faded away. Why he had repeated the insulting rhyme, he didn't know. Perhaps it was to prove he had as much bravado as the Payne boys. Perhaps it was to find out what the snailman would do; the very thought sent a tingle of fear and excitement racing up and down his spine.

The dog growled, undecided whether to take on this nervous newcomer. The regular *click, click* of the shuttle ceased and the man rose abruptly, his brow creased in a questioning furrow. Clearly the unfamiliar, hesitant voice intrigued him and he stood in the doorway, glaring at Timothy. His face was hard and forbidding, the skin coarse, the features bluntly cut. His nose had obviously been broken earlier in life and badly reset, giving him the belligerent expression of a prizefighter. One of his eyes was misformed, and it rolled around menacingly under a lowered lid. But with the other, the good eye, he looked intently, penetratingly at the boy.

Timothy stopped in mid-verse, uncertain whether to run or stay, to laugh or cry. For a long time, the snailman stared at him and through him and then, turning away, he said softly to the growling dog, "Take it easy, Crabby. He don't mean no harm to you or me."

The huge man haunted Timothy's thoughts and strode through his dreams. Night after night the boy woke in a sweat, with one coldly penetrating eye boring into his skull. He wanted to go back, to see him again, to prove to himself that the snailman was a human being, made of bones and blood, and not some phantom of his own making. And he had behaved very badly, he knew that all too well. Chanting the stupid rhyme at the snailman and then slinking away, shuffling back down the lane with his tail between his legs, was a cowardly thing to do. He wanted to apologize, to speak to the man in an open, honest way, but the snailman had assumed fearful proportions in his mind. Many times he set off toward the house on Carpenters' Hill, only to lose courage and drag himself home again.

"What's Bob the snailman's real name?" he asked his parents.

"Minns or Mimms, I think," said his father, who was busily sketching.

"Why?" said his mother, drawing her brows together in a frown. "Have you been seeing him?"

"I saw him . , . once," said Timothy.

"Well, don't go near him again, please."

"Why not?"

"Yes, why not, dear?" repeated Mr. Eden.

"Oh, you know," said his wife, with one of her "don't let's talk about it in front of the child" looks that Timothy knew so well.

Mr. Eden shrugged.

"There are plenty of other people—I mean children—for you to play with, darling," said Mrs. Eden, in a coaxing kind of voice.

"There isn't anyone," pouted Timothy.

"What about the Paynes? They live close by."

Timothy looked aghast. Didn't his mother know? Didn't she have eyes in her head?

"Horrible brats," commented Mr. Eden, endorsing his son's opinion and, seeing Timothy's downcast expression, he pulled the boy toward him. "You're really fed up, aren't you? Missing all your old friends in London?"

Timothy nuzzled into his father's neck to hide the tears that were stinging his eyes.

"Never mind," said Mr. Eden, stroking the boy's long brown hair. "You'll soon make friends here. It's just a matter of getting used to a new place. It isn't easy. I never said it would be, did I?"

Timothy stole a sideways glance at his mother. She was sitting at the table, her head bent over her sewing so that he could hardly see her face. But her hands moved jerkily, the needle jabbing in and out of the cloth until, inevitably, it pierced her finger and she said something under her breath. Moving to the country had not pleased her either, though she tried to hide her feelings from her son.

"Anyway"—Mr. Eden shook Timothy's shoulders in a cheering up kind of way—"you'll be going to Shrewsbury next year and there'll be so much to do you probably won't want to come back here for holidays to see your poor old dad and mother."

Timothy's heart sank even further, but not for worlds would he have admitted that the prospect of going to boarding school was infinitely worse than the horrible little school in the village. At least he could crawl back every night to the warmth of his home, hide in his own little room and feel safe . . . for a while. At boarding school there would be no escape, no peace day or night, either in the schoolroom or the dormitory. Always there would be other boys around, and some of them would be, had to be, just as rotten as the Payne brothers. He shuddered at the thought. But Shrewsbury was his father's old school, and his grandfather's. The Edens had been going there since the school was founded, as far as Timothy could make out, and it would have been unthinkable for him to look his father in the eye and say, "Dad, I don't want to go."

On the other hand, he pondered, as he moped around the garden later that afternoon, could it really be as bad as the village school? The children there all hated him. They mimicked his accent, called him a foreigner. "But I'm an Englishman," he had retorted, in amazement.

"English . . . bah!" they jeered. "You're a toffee-nosed Londoner. We don't want no la-dee-dah Londoners 'ere."

To make it worse, he was brighter than the other children of his age and the principal had put him into a higher class . . . with the eleven-year-olds. Though Timothy wasn't small, most of the children in the new class were bigger than he, so the toffee-nosed Londoner also became the "little runt."

It was great sport for them to gather round him during playtimes and jeer. "Never did like midgets." They'd nudge each other and point at the red-faced boy who did his best to pretend he couldn't hear their insults.

" 'E's some kind of a freak, 'f yer ask me. I could squash 'im with me foot . . . like a worm."

"D'yer think 'e'll ever grow up normal?" they would ask each other with feigned innocence.

"Nah. Not a 'ope. 'E's a weirdo. 'E'll be stunted like that all 'is life."

"Little runt! Little runt! Little runt!"

The more aggressive children, like the Paynes, ganged up on him and pummeled and kicked him till a teacher arrived and put a stop to it.

"What happened this time?" his mother would say, looking at her bruised and battered son when he got home. But Timothy said nothing.

"They're giving you a bad time, aren't they, old boy?" said his father sadly. "They're a lot of damned little bullies."

"Ssh, Roger!" reprimanded his wife. "Don't swear in front of—" and she pointed at Timothy's head.

"I don't care," retorted Mr. Eden. "I detest bullies."

His parents were fighting again. Timothy could hear them from his perch in the horse chestnut tree. They never shouted or raged. Instead they hissed at each other in small, explosive whispers so that Timothy supposedly wouldn't hear. Of late, it had been the same old quarrel repeated over and over.

"Well, *you* wanted to come," hissed his mother. "I would have been quite happy to stay where we were."

"What? Live in that wretched little flat in suburbia all our miserable lives?" fumed his father. "That was no life!"

"And I suppose you think this is," came the whispered reply. "Living in the back of beyond, with no friends and nothing to do . . ."

"There's plenty to do, if you'll only look around."

"Like what, Roger? Dishing out cucumber sandwiches at the vicarage tea or tatting with the ladies at the sewing circle?" she snarled. "It's all right for you. You've got your work. But what have I got? I can't get a job. There's nothing in this Godforsaken place."

17

"You could look further afield. You could try in Thurbridge or . . ."

"I have tried . . . everywhere," she interrupted him impatiently. "Remember, I don't have a car to get around. I'm stuck here all the time . . . rotting away with boredom."

Timothy put his hands over his ears, trying to blot out the angry exchange. He knew this move to the country was a bone of contention between his parents and he was afraid. Mothers and fathers had a nasty habit of splitting up—it had happened

18

to some of his school friends—and Timothy often crept out of bed at night, when he heard the hissing start in his parents' bedroom, and prayed fervently to God that He would keep them together . . . at least until he grew up. The only person who had wanted to move was his father. "We can't stay in this overcrowded city for the rest of our lives," he had explained to Timothy. "I want you to grow up in the country, just as I did, where the air is fresh and you're not jostled by crowds everywhere you go."

It had distressed Mrs. Eden, who resented leaving her family and friends. As for Timothy, he had looked forward to it, the way one looks forward to a holiday by the sea, until the day arrived when all his possessions were piled into a big moving van and he waved good-bye to Michael Sanders and Christopher Lyons and the girl who lived opposite and the old lady in the sweet shop . . . and everyone.

"If that's the way you feel about it . . ." Mr. Eden's exasperated voice penetrated Timothy's thoughts, bringing him back to the present with a jolt. "Go back to London! I don't care!"

"Don't push me, Roger, because I just might do that! I just might!" came the angry reply.

Timothy slid down the tree trunk, scraping his hands and knees, but he didn't care. He had to get away. Away from the nightmare that was fast becoming reality. He ran across the garden and out into the lane. He ran and ran until he was out of breath. When he finally stopped, he realized he was halfway up Carpenters' Hill and very close to the snailman's cottage. He hesitated. Back down the hill was his home, where his parents were quarreling. Up at the top of the hill was the strange man, the weird one. Timothy went on.

The dog saw him first. He was lying on his side on the cold, wet earth, his eyes half closed, lost in a dream world of rabbits and bones, but when he saw the stranger, his eyes snapped open.

The door of the house was closed and the snailman nowhere in sight.

Timothy knelt down. "Hello, Crabby," he whispered as softly as he could.

The dog growled, a tiny warning growl at the back of its throat that said, "No trespassers . . . or else!"

The boy put his hand through the bars of the gate and made little clicking noises with his fingers to entice the dog. "Come on, Crabby," he whispered. "You're only pretending to be fierce, old fellow."

The dog rose to his feet and stood, unsure, half-wagging his tail, waving his head from side to side in an agony of uncertainty.

"Come on Crabby, good boy," crooned Timothy, willing the dog to come to him. The dog took a few steps and stopped.

"Go on, you mangy old cur," boomed a deep voice a few feet from where Timothy knelt. "You got no reason to be scared o' nobody."

Timothy was so surprised, he fell backward, landing on his elbows. The next moment, the snailman himself reared into view, and, leaning on the gate, he peered down at the small, frightened boy.

"You got no reason to be scared neither," he said, and his one good eye looked kindly at Timothy. But the other one, sunken under its heavy, half-closed lid, gave the face a mean expression. Timothy tried not to look at it.

"I . . . I . . . ," he began, looking up into the face as if he were mesmerized by it. Crabby, more confident now, poked a wet nose through the bars and sniffed at him.

"Come in," said the snailman, unlocking the gate and pulling it open a foot or two.

Timothy scrambled to his feet and sidled in, flattening himself against the gatepost so as not to get too close to the man. He felt as if he were going to the dentist, and similar emotions welled up in him: fear, confusion, a terrible urge to run.

Once Timothy was inside the gate, Crabby gave him a thorough sniffing and promptly lost interest, loping off after his master. For the first time, Timothy realized the snailman was slightly crippled. Nobody had told him that, not even his nosy informants in the village had mentioned that Bob Mimms had some kind of a spinal deformity that gave him a lurching, one-sided gait.

The dog and the man disappeared into the house and Timothy stood, hesitating, too embarrassed to leave—it would be unthinkably childish to run away now—but too timid to go on. For one long, miserable moment, he thought he might spend the rest of his life standing there, rooted to the spot, a monument to indecision, until the snailman appeared in the doorway and beckoned to him.

The interior of the cottage was a surprise. Timothy's father often referred to some of his colleagues as "smelly old bachelors," men who lived alone and didn't care too much about cleaning floors and washing dishes, but the snailman wasn't like that. His little home was clean and relatively tidy. Not spotless, Timothy decided, the way his aunt's house was, with every cushion plumped up and lots of glass ornaments ready to fall on the floor and smash into tiny pieces as soon as a person even looked at them, but comfortable and bright with homey, rough-hewn furniture and hand-woven rugs on the floor.

"Bun?" said the snailman.

"Huh?" Timothy was so nervous it had even affected his hearing.

The man opened an earthenware jar and produced a sticky, very curranty bun. Timothy's eyes lit up and he reached out for the bun, mumbling his thanks.

"Bun?" said the man again, looking at Crabby, who immediately sat up on his haunches and began to drool.

The bun was delicious and the cottage cosy and the dog fun . . . and the snailman wasn't so terrible after all, decided

Timothy, sneaking a quick look at the giant now and then when he was quite sure he wasn't aware of it. The boy wondered where all the snails were. From the way people talked, he had expected to see snails all over the house, climbing up the walls and across the ceilings . . . but there wasn't one in sight.

Perhaps it was all a joke, he thought, one of those grown-up jokes he never seemed to understand.

The man pointed to an overstuffed, chintz-covered armchair and indicated that Timothy should sit in it, while he lowered

himself, painfully, Timothy noticed, onto a high-backed chair before the open fire.

Crabby finished his bun and so did Timothy. And then the three of them just sat, Crabby gazing into space, the snailman staring at the crackling logs in the fireplace and Timothy, who didn't know what to do with himself, fidgeting and picking at hangnails and running his hands through his hair a thousand times. When he went visiting alone, or with his parents, people made conversation. They said, "How are you?" and "Do you like school?" and "What do you want to be when you grow up?" and when he had answered all three inevitable questions, the conversation was usually over . . . for him . . . except for a comment or two about how tall he was growing.

But this man didn't ask questions.

After a while, Timothy's embarrassment became quite unbearable and he blurted out, "I'm ten. I'll be eleven in October."

Crabby yawned and lay down and the snailman picked up a poker and worried the glowing logs. Then he sat back with a grunt and folded his great gnarled hands in his lap.

Timothy swallowed hard. "How old are *you*?" he said. He had a nasty suspicion that wasn't the right kind of question to ask an adult, but this adult didn't seem to behave according to the normal rules anyway.

"Reckon I'm forty-eight or fifty . . . something like that."

"You can't be," Timothy retorted, and instantly regretted it. It was unwise to say, "You can't," to anyone the size of the snailman. One of his hands was bigger than Timothy's head, and with his two hands he could have crushed the life out of him.

"I mean," he mumbled, "you . . . people, that is, are usually one age or another."

"My parents died when I was just a young 'un, like you." The snailman kept staring into the fire. "They never told me how old I were . . . and there were nobody else to tell me neither."

"No aunts or uncles?" said Timothy, who couldn't imagine a family without the full complement of godmothers, uncles, and cousins.

The man shook his head. "Jus' me. There weren't even ol' Crabby in those days."

"You've always lived alone here?"

He nodded. "I don't like people . . . leastways, not many o' them."

"Oh."

There wasn't much else to say. Not on that subject anyway. Timothy had a feeling it was wrong to say you didn't like people. "There's some good in everyone, if you'll only look for it," his mother told him, but Timothy had met people who didn't seem to have an ounce of good in them, even if you examined them under a microscope. People like the Payne brothers. Try as he might, Timothy could find nothing worth-while in those brutish louts.

The silence descended again. Nothing stirred. No clock ticked. No pots and pans clattered in the kitchen. No television droned on and on.

"We've just moved here from Croydon," said Timothy, unable to bear the quietness a moment longer. "We live in Stourley now, in the village . . . well, not right in the village, actually, our house is in Orchard Lane, right next to the Thompsons. Do you know Mr. Thompson?" Timothy rushed on, neither expecting nor receiving an answer. "He's really old, about a hundred, I think, and he's lived in that house all his life. He told me so. He collects butterflies . . . they're beautiful . . . he's got them in glass cases all around his study and . . ." He shot a glance at the snailman. What else could he say? What else could he do to fill the heavy silence? "My father's a medical illustrator," he continued relentlessly. "He does drawings of parts of the body for doctors' books and my mother used to be a secretary in London but she can't get a job in the village because there aren't any companies and she's very bored and . . ." He realized he was babbling. And the man wasn't listening anyway. Timothy screwed his hands be-tween his knees and wished he could find a way of saying he wanted to leave. Perhaps he could just slip out, he thought, since the snailman wasn't paying any attention to him. Neither was Crabby. He was snoring. There had to be something he could talk about, Timothy thought desperately, something that would interest the snailman.

"Where are you . . . uhm . . . where are the snails?" he asked in a very hesitant voice, because everybody laughed about Bob Mimms's snails and he didn't want the man to think he was laughing too.

The snailman stirred and, again with a wince of pain, heaved himself out of the chair. Without a word, he went out of the house and opened the door of a small whitewashed shed. Timothy followed, uninvited, his curiosity overcoming any timidity. Inside it was cool and damp, rather like stepping into a cave by the sea.

"Careful!" commanded the man, pointing at the floor. Five or six very large snails were gliding across the damp earth, their tentacles weaving from side to side in an inquisitive way.

Timothy trod carefully. The thought of stepping on one of the slimy creatures turned his stomach over. Then he realized they were on the walls and ceilings too, dozens of them, clinging like limpets. What if one were to lose its hold and fall on him, its cold, wet body slithering over his flesh, maybe disappearing down the back of his neck? He shuddered involuntarily and buttoned up his collar, hunching his shoulders to protect himself against any sudden onslaught. A shelf ran down one side of the room with a ridge a few inches high. Timothy peered over the top. It was covered with dock leaves and moss, pieces of lettuce and decaying vegetables. About

thirty snails were in various stages of activity—eating, gliding slowly across the vegetable mat, or sleeping. Mostly they were sleeping.

"They're huge," said Timothy, admiring a particularly big one.

The man nodded solemnly. "That's Jake," he said, stroking the snail affectionately with his great, scaly finger, as if it were a puppy or kitten.

"Do they all have names?"

"Of course."

"Why?"

"Why not?" The man stared at him, his good eye beginning to look as forbidding as the other one, and Timothy quickly changed the subject. "I've never seen such big snails," he said. "We only have tiddly little ones in the garden at home."

"I breeds 'em like that," said Bob Mimms, gently removing one from the wall and placing it on a lettuce leaf. "The small ones I throws out."

"What do you do with them?" Timothy remembered visiting a very posh restaurant in London once, with his godfather. "Do you eat them?"

The good eye gave him an even sterner look.

Timothy blushed and started to stroke the nearest snail in a jerky manner. Outside, Crabby was whining and scratching at the door.

"He don't come in here," said the man, as Timothy made a move to let the dog in. "He steps on 'em with those great paws of his. See those two." He pointed to a pair glued together at the back of the shelf. "They're mating. Three weeks' time there'll be eighty or ninety littl'uns."

"Eighty or ninety!" Timothy's eyes popped. That was a lot of babies in one fell swoop.

"They don't . . ." Timothy swallowed. He realized he had to be very careful with his words or the snailman would think he was criticizing his pets or, worse still, making fun of them. "They don't do very much, do they? I mean . . . ," he quickly qualified his statement, "they don't move around . . . or play."

The man turned abruptly and left the outbuilding, pushing Crabby to one side as he opened the door.

Timothy was mortified. Had he offended him again, he wondered miserably? But the next moment the snailman reappeared, carrying a length of hose, which he attached to a tap in the corner.

"Watch!" he commanded, turning on the tap and adjusting the head of the hose to a very fine spray. "They thinks it's rain."

Sure enough, every snail perked up and started to move around. Tentacles swayed, shells wobbled, bodies undulated.

"It must be difficult moving around like that," suggested Timothy. "Like trying to walk on your stomach."

"It ain't a stomach. It's one big foot . . . look!" the snailman said, tipping a snail upside down for Timothy to see.

Timothy resisted the temptation to say "Ugh!" and wrinkle his nose. But the man must have sensed the boy's repugnance.

"They have a right to live," he said quietly, looking all the while at the small creature in his hand. "They don't harm nobody. They ain't so pretty to look at, but neither are we. Leastways, I ain't. . . ."

He returned the snail to its place on the shelf and opened the shed door. "Come on," he said to the dog, who was waiting patiently for him and, as an afterthought he added, "Goodbye," to Timothy.

Timothy gulped. Usually people built up to a leavetaking with "I must go now," "Thank you for the lovely tea," "Oh, can't you stay a little longer? No? Oh dear, well, do come again soon . . . promise?"

But the snailman didn't bother with convention. And he hadn't said, "Come again." Timothy stood and looked at the closed door for some time and then he turned and wandered back to the gate, deep in thought.

"Been a-visitin', young man?" said a voice close by.

Timothy jumped.

"I'm sorry I startled you," said Mr. Thompson, Timothy's neighbor in Orchard Lane. His old face creased into a thousand lines as he laughed at the boy's confusion.

"I've been to see . . ."

"Bob Mimms," said the old man, and Timothy realized it was the first time he had ever heard anyone call the snailman by his proper name. "What did you think of him?"

"He seemed"—Timothy searched for the word—"all right," he finished lamely.

31

"Course he is," agreed Mr. Thompson, shuffling slowly down the steep hill with the aid of a cherry-wood walking stick. "But folk round here have taken against him. Just because he's not pretty to look at . . . and he keeps hisself to hisself."

"He doesn't like people."

"Got no reason to neither. Ever since his mum and dad passed away, he's had to go it alone. Nobody's ever helped him, poor little fellow," said the old man. "Just a nipper he were then. Now look at him . . . a great oak tree." He shook his head. "But he suffers something terrible with that back of his. Hit by a car he was, many years ago. Back's never been the same since. Some days he's fair bent over, just like me, but I'm nearly ninety and he's still a young man."

He paused, waiting for a suitable comment from the boy.

Timothy recalled his mother's standard remarks on similar occasions.

"You certainly don't look your age," he said obligingly. Mr. Thompson appeared to be pleased with the empty compliment.

"My wife Flora, she's ten years younger than me, but she has terrible trouble with her feet. Bunions, she has, the size of Spanish onions, you wouldn't believe it . . ." and he rambled on, while Timothy let his mind wander away. He was back in the house on the hill, watching the huge man as he touched his pets, lovingly, gently, as if they were his children.

"He's got some huge snails there," said Timothy, and realized too late he had interrupted Mr. Thompson in mid-flight about his latest operation in the cottage hospital. The old man's mouth fell open and he was clearly struggling mentally with the transition from hernias to snails.

"I've never seen them," he said. "Don't want to neither. I've got quite enough of the dratted things in me garden, up and down the irises. Bob Mimms should stick to his weavin'. At least it earns him a livin'. Lady come by a few years back

33

and sees him weavin' away like he always do and she says, 'Oh, how lovely,' she says, and buys everythin' he makes. Sells it in her shop in Bournemouth, so I hear tell."

"So he . . . so he doesn't cadge and rob?"

"Lord no!" the old man frowned at the very suggestion. "That's just a stupid rhyme made up by folk who should know better. I tell you, laddie," he added, with an indignant snort, "if everybody kept hisself to hisself and worked as hard as Bob Mimms, the world would be a better place for it."

Finally they arrived at Mr. Thompson's gate and he laid a friendly hand on the boy's shoulder. "Come in and have tea with us soon," he said. "My wife enjoys company."

Timothy shuffled from one foot to the other. He had a special favor to ask of the old man, but he didn't want to say, "Please don't tell my mother I went to see the snailman," because that sounded sneaky. At the same time, he reasoned, there was no point in getting her upset about nothing.

"Mr. Thompson," he said at last, "My mother doesn't like Bob Mimms . . . I mean, well, she's never actually met him . . . but she's heard funny things about him and . . ." his voice trailed away. He wasn't doing very well.

The old man chuckled. "I won't tell her I see you up there today, Timmy. It'll be a secret 'tween you and me," and he drew a finger across his throat in a very conspiratorial manner. "Oh dear!" he muttered, opening his gate quickly and slamming it shut behind him. "Here comes Rennet Miller. I don't want nothing to do with the likes of him," and he staggered up the path to his front door as fast as his arthritic old legs would carry him.

Timothy turned to see who Rennet Miller might be. A tramp, he thought, judging by the man's unkempt appearance and straggly beard, probably coming to ask for money or food, which explained why old Thompson had taken off in such a hurry. He smiled to himself and ran into his house shouting, "Mum! Dad! Where are you?"

"Up here, darling," called his mother. "We're painting the back bedroom. It looks so . . ." But the shrill ringing of the doorbell interrupted her. "Will you answer it, Timothy, please."

He opened the door and was surprised to see the tramp standing there despite the "No hawkers, no circulars," sign on the garden gate.

"Good aft'noon, young gen'leman," he said in a silky voice. "Is the lady of the 'ouse at 'ome?"

"Yes, who is it?" said Mrs. Eden, running down the stairs and wiping her hands on a towel.

"Good aft'noon, ma'am. Fine weather we are 'avin' for the time of the year."

Close up, Rennet Miller was even more shabby, Timothy decided, and he had a horrible smell about him, a smell that suggested soap and water were his sworn enemies. He wore a dirty old cardigan, obviously beloved by moths, over an even dirtier old shirt. His trousers were smeared with paint and dung and tied up like sacks under his knees. But his clothing,

35

offensive as it was, was nowhere as repulsive as the man himself.

He held his hat obsequiously in front of him, in what was meant to be an ingratiating gesture, but his mouth twisted in a contemptuous leer and his eyes, shifty and sly, were keen as a fox's.

"What can I do for you?" said Mrs. Eden, in the curt voice she reserved for door-to-door salesmen . . . or her son when he misbehaved.

"Me name is Rennet Miller, ma'am." He paused, as if the name should mean something, but, receiving no response, he pressed on. "You do 'ave a real lovely garden 'ere," he said, turning to admire it.

"Yes, well . . ."

"I'm a gardener, you see. First class. I've got all me references 'ere," and he started to pull some dog-eared pieces of paper out of his pocket.

"Thank you," said Mrs. Eden quickly. "But we really don't need the services of a gardener."

The man's mouth tightened and he moved a step or two closer. "Oh, but I think as 'ow you do, ma'am," he said in a very insolent way. "That there pear tree needs prunin' and you've got crabgrass and a touch o' blight in the . . ."

"Thank you. No."

Rennet Miller's eyes narrowed.

"He has the meanest face I've ever seen," thought Timothy, and he shuddered involuntarily.

"I come quite cheap, ma'am," he insisted and put his foot in the door as Mrs. Eden made to shut it.

Timothy backed away, afraid.

"I been out o' work for a long time," persisted Rennet Miller, pushing the door open abruptly and glaring at Mrs. Eden. "I need money, 'n' if I don't get some soon . . ."

"Roger! Roger, please come here a moment!" Mrs. Eden called out, trying to keep the panic out of her voice.

"What is it?" said Mr. Eden, pounding down the stairs.

"Good day, ma'am," said Rennet Miller and, with a smile that was more a snarl, he turned and shambled away.

"Horrible man," Mrs. Eden shivered, shutting the door.

"A tramp," said her husband comfortingly. "He's harmless."

"That man . . . Rennet something . . . he's horrible," Timothy protested to Mr. Thompson the next day. "Do you know, he threatened my mother."

"Call the police," said the old man, sucking vociferously on his false teeth. "That's what you should've done. Call the police."

"Well, we . . ."

"I won't have him on my property, no I won't!" interrupted Mr. Thompson, warming to the subject. "He did some gardenin' for me once. Gardenin'! Huh!" the old man scoffed. "Ruined me plum trees he did, and as for me azaleas, he cut off all their . . ."

"But who is he . . . where does he live?" said Timothy quickly. Mr. Thompson could get very boring on the subject of his azaleas.

"He don't live nowhere, 'cept in hedges and ditches. Old Bob took pity on him a while back, let him stay at his place for a night or two, but Rennet hurt that there dog of his,

Crabby, and Bob gave him a good thrashin' and sent him off
with a flea in his ear . . . so I hear tell."

"Is Rennet from the village?"

"Lord bless you, no!" The old man prickled with indignation. "He turned up like a bad penny 'bout six months ago,
pretendin' to look for work. Said he was a gardener. A gardener!
He wouldn't know one end of a shovel from the other!" he
sniffed contemptuously and gave his teeth another vigorous
suck. "Ruined me plum tree, he did, and as for azaleas, he
cut off all their . . ."

Timothy sighed.

On Friday afternoons Miss Forfar always gave her class a
general knowledge quiz. It was meant to be a fairly light-
hearted, enjoyable half-hour to finish off the week. It didn't
really matter whether the children scored high or low and Miss
Forfar's mouth didn't disappear into a thin, angry line if someone gave a silly answer.

At the beginning, Timothy had enjoyed the quizzes and his
hand had always been the first to shoot up. Often his was the
only hand and Miss Forfar would beam, "Well done, Timothy."

But the other children turned hostile faces toward him and
he could read hatred in their eyes.

"Know-it-all," snarled Harry Payne, jostling him as they
left the schoolroom.

Outside the gate a dozen or so from his class had gathered

to taunt him. "Well done, Timothy. Oh well done," they jeered, mimicking Miss Forfar's clipped Scottish accent.

Somebody took a swing and hit him on the shoulder. Timothy spun round, eyes blazing. "Now, look here . . . ," he began, but a blow from behind caught him on the head and sent him flying.

"Well done, Timothy. Oh, well done," sang the chorus, as he dragged himself to his feet and brushed his dirty, bloody knees, and then the inevitable "Toffee-nosed Londoner. Thinks he's somethin' special, he do. . . ."

"And what is the highest mountain in the British Isles?" Miss Forfar asked the following Friday afternoon. She looked questioningly around the room. "Does nobody have the answer? Timothy?" She was perplexed by his silence. "Surely you know, Timothy?" but he shook his head and kept his eyes glued to the desk.

Of course he knew. He had known the answer to that old chestnut for years, but wild horses wouldn't have dragged it from him now.

Harry Payne sniggered and kicked him from behind. Timothy turned round to retaliate, but Miss Forfar had seen the incident

"Harry Payne," she said, her voice icy with contempt, "leave the room. When you can behave in a civilized manner you may return. But I'm afraid that will be a long, long time. . . ." And she gave him a withering look.

"I'll get you for that, you rotten scum," whispered Fatty Simons.

Outside the schoolroom, Harry Payne hunted with his two brothers. But in school his special pal was Fatty Simons, a loathsome boy, with flame-colored hair, cut as short as a scrubbing brush, and a body that would have looked at home on a baby hippo.

Fatty lived right opposite the schoolhouse, in a tumbledown shack inhabited by his mother, eleven brothers and sisters, and assorted scruffy dogs and cats. His father had disappeared long ago. "And I don't blame him," said Timothy's own father the first time he saw Mrs. Simons.

Harry and Fatty had made it their business to spearhead the attack on the "toffee-nosed Londoner" and they lost no opportunity for making his life unbearable.

"Just wait till school's over," snarled Fatty, scowling at Timothy from the other side of the aisle. "I'll get you."

"And I'll get you, you tub of lard," shot back Timothy, who at that moment was ready to take on anyone or anything to put an end to his misery.

Meanwhile, Miss Forfar was busily explaining how pygmies hunted in the jungles of Africa.

"Are there any questions?" she concluded, closing her books with an end-of-the-week finality, but her question was swallowed up in the noise of chairs being scraped back and desks slammed shut. It was three-thirty, right on the button, and anybody who dared to ask a question would have been in trouble from the rest of the class.

But Timothy was already in trouble. The crowd of sullen faces gathered round the gate made that very clear to him.

Harry Payne stood foursquare, his arms crossed, the light of battle in his eyes. "You nasty little creep," he growled as Timothy drew level. "I'm goin' to rearrange your face."

Timothy threw his satchel to the ground and took off his coat. Though his heart was pounding and his mouth dry as chalk, he was determined to stand and fight it out.

"Okay," he said, glaring at the Payne boy and raising his fists. "Come on!"

Harry Payne stepped back, his eyelids fluttering nervously. He didn't intend, had never intended, to take Timothy on in single combat. He looked round quickly for support, but the others hung back, intimidated by the look in Timothy's eye and his tightly clenched fists.

Harry Payne's hesitation and the obvious cowardice of his gang of supporters gave Timothy the spurt of courage he needed. Seizing his opportunity, he rushed forward, flailing about him wildly with fists and feet. Surprised shouts and squeals of pain rang out and his tormentors broke rank and fled. So did Timothy, across the main London-to-Bournemouth road, without even looking, though his mother had warned him about it a hundred times, and down Carpenters' Hill as fast as he could go.

He had managed to get away but he knew he could never win against them, not six or seven boys bigger and stronger than he. He also knew they would quickly regain their courage and follow him. Which they did. He could hear them now, their boots banging against the road, their voices raised in excited shouts.

"Let's get the little swine! Kill the creep!"

Harry Payne's voice was louder than the rest.

They were gaining on him and Timothy was growing tired.

He would never make it to his home, never. He would have to stop and fight again. And then, as he rounded a corner, a marvelous idea occurred to him. Putting on an extra spurt, he reached the snailman's gate and clambered over.

The rest of the pack arrived, red-faced and panting. They drew up sharply when they saw Timothy inside the gate, and looked at each other, uncertain what to do.

"We can't go in there," mumbled one, shuffling his feet nervously. "Ol' Bob'll kill us." And he pointed to the "Private. Keep out!" notice on the tree.

Timothy's heart leaped. He was safe. He would wait for them to go away, as they surely would, and then he would leave before the snailman came out and found him trespassing on his property.

"Well, what about 'im then?" Harry Payne glared at Timothy, disappointed at losing his prey. "'E's in there 'n' nobody's killed 'im yet, far as I can see."

"Let's get 'im," said Fatty Simons, putting his foot on the bottom bar of the gate as if to climb over, and they all sprang forward like hounds after a cornered fox.

Timothy closed his eyes and waited for the inevitable assault. But nothing happened. Tentatively he opened them again and saw the boys huddled together, staring past him with angry yet fearful looks.

He turned and followed the direction of their eyes. The snailman was coming down the path, a mad look in his eye, his fists clenched till the muscles stood out like great branches. He seemed to be growling or muttering under his breath.

"Trapped," thought Timothy, feeling faint.

A hand descended on his shoulder, a hand so big and so heavy Timothy thought he would sink under the weight of it.

Whole years of his life slipped by while he stood with that hand gripping his shoulder. Nothing was said. Not a word. The crowd of ruffians beyond the gate lowered their eyes and shuffled from foot to foot. Then, muttering curses and vague threats, they slunk away.

Timothy realized he was shaking. He stole a glance up, up at the man towering over him.

The snailman returned his look. "Bun?" he said.

Timothy gave him a wobbly smile. And the two walked into the house together.

Later that evening Miss Forfar phoned to say she had found his coat and satchel. Timothy didn't know what else she had said, but when he hung up his father looked angry and flushed.

"I'm going round to talk to Mr. Payne," he snapped, pulling on a coat. "This bullying has got to stop or I'll give his boys a thrashing myself."

"No, don't, Dad." Timothy grabbed his father's arm. "Please," he pleaded. "Bullies are weaklings. They're not worth bothering about."

A strange expression passed over Mr. Eden's face and he touched his son lightly on the cheek. "You're really growing up, old man," he said, in a wondering kind of way. "I'm proud of you, you know."

Timothy didn't tell him that the words were not his. They were something the snailman had said that afternoon, when Timothy had told him about the boys at the village school. "A bully's a coward in his heart, but he don't want nobody to know it," the snailman had replied, and Timothy had nodded, knowing he was right.

Then he had sat cross-legged, in front of the fire, a bun in one hand, the other stroking the soft fur above Crabby's eyes. And he had talked. He had told the snailman about his sadness at leaving his old home and about the spiteful children in his class. He had even told him about his parents' quarrels and his deep-down terror that they might leave each other . . . and him. He had never breathed a word about that to anyone—it was childish and he was ashamed of it—but the snailman had simply listened and nodded. And, somehow, Timothy had felt comforted.

The snailman had not said "Come again" when he left. But Timothy went anyway. Almost every day, on his way home from school, and always at weekends.

Most of the time, the snailman was weaving. He sat for hours at the small loom, casting the shuttle back and forth, back and forth, while Crabby lay beside him, dreamily watching as the lengths of brightly colored, delicately patterned fabric cascaded from the loom onto the floor. "May I try?" said Timothy one day. The snailman stopped his rhythmical movement and put his hands on the loom as if it were a beloved child.

"I never let nobody touch it," he said protectively.

"I'll be very careful, I promise," Timothy pleaded. The man looked at his loom, then at the boy's eager face, then at his loom again. He frowned, as if he were going through some kind of inner turmoil. "All right," he said grudgingly. "Sit here." And he got up to make way for Timothy. "But don't you touch nothin' till I tells you," he admonished.

Then, patiently, he explained to the boy the ancient art of weaving.

"Reckon you'd be good at it," he said after a while, watching Timothy make his first tentative attempts with the shuttle. "But you'll have to practice. Nothin' comes easy. Least of all weavin'. It's somethin' . . . somethin' special." And he touched the little loom reverently.

When Timothy wasn't in the cottage watching the snailman weaving, or playing tug o' war with Crabby, he spent his time in the outbuilding with the snails. He took lettuce from his garden for them, making sure that his mother didn't see him. When she finally noticed the great holes in the lettuce patch, she said, "Those wretched rabbits!" And Timothy didn't contradict her.

He spent hours in the snail shed, sometimes with Bob Mimms, sometimes alone. He discovered that snails were different from each other, just like people. Some had dark shells, some light, some were fat, others lean, some had long tentacles, others short, some moved around a lot . . . for snails . . . others slept most of the time. Timothy picked them up

47

and laughed at the way they scrunched themselves tightly into their shells, fearful, cowering. One memorable day he determined to overcome his fear of their cold, slimy bodies and picking up Jake, the biggest, he put the snail in the palm of his hand and squeezed his eyes shut, dreading the feel of its body as it emerged from its shell.

Jake seemed equally uneasy about the whole thing, for he stayed firmly entrenched.

Timothy opened his eyes cautiously and felt a pang of disappointment that the snail had not responded to his overtures of friendship.

"Perhaps *he* doesn't like the touch of *my* skin," he thought. And the realization startled him.

At last, after a long, patient wait on Timothy's part, the snail ventured out, its tentacles quivering doubtfully.

"It's okay, Jake," Timothy whispered, trying to sound as encouraging as he could. "It's okay, old boy. I won't hurt you. You know that." And he felt something akin to gratitude when the snail finally emerged and glided gracefully across the palm of his hand.

In time, Timothy came to know all the snails by name. Not only Jake, but Ted, Jimmy, Albert, Ernest, and Thompson. "Thompson?"

"After ol' Mr. Thompson," the snailman explained, " 'cos they're both old and doddery." And he laughed, a rare laugh that lit up his good eye and made the mean one look even meaner, as if it hadn't understood the joke.

48

They began to race the snails, Timothy backing Jake, his favorite, because he was so wide awake, and Bob touting for Ted: "He's slow but he always gets there in the end."

Jake was a skittish young snail. He would set off down the track at a good pace, at least eight centimeters a minute, and then something would distract him, a succulent piece of boiled potato or a slice of decaying beet. Meanwhile the snailman's personal champion was undulating down the track, a sure winner. Sometimes the race took hours, with Jake weaving all over the shelf and up the walls and Ted retiring into his shell for a nap. The snailman glared and called them all the danged idiots and Timothy laughed until the tears rolled down his cheeks.

Timothy often wondered at the gentleness of the snailman. He handled everything—his loom, his snails, his dog—with a touch that belied his great strength.

"Don't do that!" he had said angrily one day as Timothy hurled a stone at a crow.

"But they eat the crops."

"They don't eat the crops. They eat food, just like you 'n me. You think we should give 'em a ration book or somethin'?"

Another day Timothy discovered a rabbit crouching in the corner of the snailman's kitchen, his foreleg splinted and bandaged.

"Found him in the lane," said Bob, in answer to Timothy's question. "Danged car hit him. . . ."

The rabbit watched Crabby warily, jumping and twitching every time the dog moved. But Crabby ignored him. Live and let live was his philosophy too.

One afternoon, as he strolled down Carpenters' Hill, Timothy heard a scuffling in the field behind the hedgerow. Intrigued, thinking it might be a hare or something even bigger, he ran to the nearest gate and, climbing up the crossbars, he leaned over until he could see well into the field.

A few yards down, partially hidden by the bushes, was a pile of dirty clothes . . . or so it seemed to Timothy until the pile moved and he realized it was a man. Timothy looked more closely and saw that it was Rennet Miller, the tramp who had pestered his mother for work. The man seemed to be half-sitting, half-lying in the grass, but there was a curious watchfulness about him, as if he were waiting for someone or something. Timothy waited too, curious. After a while a small bird flew on to a branch close to the tramp's head and perched there chirping merrily, looking about it in a bright inquisitive way.

Suddenly, out of the corner of his eye, Timothy saw Rennet Miller raise a catapult to his sight and, before the boy could cry out, he let fly a stone which caught the tiny bird a glancing blow.

It fell to the ground, its wings fluttering helplessly.

"Hey!" Timothy was incensed. "Hey, you . . . !" he yelled, nearly falling over the gate in his haste to get at Rennet Miller. "You stop that!" he shouted, running at the startled tramp, who hastily scrambled to his feet.

"I'll . . . I'll . . ." Timothy was beside himself with fury, but Rennet Miller reached for a stick in the undergrowth and, brandishing it about his head, he snarled at the boy, "You'll what, you little swine?"

The boy stopped in his tracks. Rennet's face was twisted in an ugly snarl, his body poised like a trapped animal ready to spring.

"You'll what?" he taunted again.

"I'll tell the police," said Timothy stoutly.

At that Rennet laughed, a horrible cackle that gurgled from the back of his throat in a menacing way. "Go on, me fine fella," he chortled. "Tell 'em. D'yer think they'll thank you fer wastin' their time? Birds!" he sneered. "Who cares about birds?" Then his expression changed abruptly and he lunged at Timothy, grabbing the boy's shoulders before he could move out of the way. "I've killed 'undreds of 'em in me time. 'Undreds, d'you 'ear?" he demanded, his stinking breath on Timothy's face. "'N' if you bothers me again, I'll kill you too!" And, spitting contemptuously on the ground, he loped away, swearing loudly and slashing at the undergrowth with the stick.

Timothy stood for a while, shaking. "Awful man! Awful man! Awful man!" he muttered over and over, waiting for his heart to stop pounding.

A pathetic fluttering nearby reminded him of the tiny bird. Moving slowly, so as not to frighten the little creature, he crept toward it.

The bird cast him a despairing look and tried to fly away. It succeeded only in lunging forward and landing beak-first in the grass. Its wing was broken, that much was obvious, and Timothy knew it could not survive very long if its sole means of transportation was hopping. He wondered what to do. He knew he should make a splint of some kind, but how and what with? And then the answer occurred to him. As gently as he could, he picked up the wounded bird and carried it to the snailman's house.

The living room was empty, the loom still. No dog bounded out to greet him.

"Anybody home?" he called. "Ain't no reason to yell like that," growled a voice from the bedroom.

Timothy frowned. The snailman was always gruff, but it was the first time Timothy had ever heard such an irritable note in his voice.

"May I come in?" he said, peering through a crack in the door.

No answer.

Timothy went in anyway.

The snailman was lying on the bed, his eyes closed, a deep frown furrowing his brow. . . .

"I found this bird," said Timothy, holding it up for the snailman to see. "I think its wing is broken. It must be in pain."

The snailman opened his eyes and scowled at him. "Ain't the only one," he muttered. "World's full o' pain."

"Would you . . . ?" began Timothy.

"Go away. Leave me in peace," came the angry answer. "And take that blasted bird with you!"

Timothy recoiled. Tears started to his eyes but he swallowed hard. Crabby, from his position at the foot of the bed, gave him a mournful look.

He crept out of the bedroom and stood looking at the small creature fluttering limply in his hands.

He felt terribly helpless.

"Crabby," he called softly, so as not to irritate the snailman again. "Here, Crabby."

The dog came with a questioning look, its paws dragging as if they were lead weights.

"Watch over it," instructed Timothy, placing the bird on the ground. "Down, Crabby. Good dog."

The dog lay down obediently and watched the bird, which immediately made a futile attempt to fly away.

"Stop him!" said Timothy and the dog, leaping after the bird, placed his long, thin snout on it, not hard enough to crush it but sufficiently hard to let it know that escape was out of the question.

Timothy stole back to the bedroom and stood hesitantly at the door. The snailman turned on his side and let out a low moan. Then his eyes opened and he saw Timothy staring at him.

"You still here?" he demanded, his good eye glaring at the boy.

"Can . . . can I get you anything?" Timothy asked. "A hot drink?"

The snailman shook his head and instantly regretted it for the pain made him wince and cry out.

"Cold," he muttered through clenched teeth.

In the cupboard Timothy found a blanket, which he threw over the snailman, tucking it in the way his mother did when she felt particularly loving. Then he stood back, unsure. He wanted to do something to relieve the man's pain but he was afraid to touch the huge misshapen body. Would the snailman resent it and lash out at him? Worse still, would he find some horrible lump or deformity on the man's back?

Overcoming his fear with an effort, Timothy reached out and, as gently as he could, he began to stroke the snailman's back. He wasn't sure where the injury was. Spinal, Mr. Thompson had said, but that could have been anywhere from the shoulder blade to the tailbone, so he rubbed somewhere between the two and hoped that it was relieving the snailman's obvious distress. He stood there for a long time, rubbing and rubbing, so long that he thought the man must have fallen asleep. When his hand felt as if it would fall off, Timothy tiptoed round the bed and, bending down, peered into the snailman's face.

The man opened his eyes and, raising his hand, placed it

on Timothy's shoulder, squeezing hard.

"You've a good heart," he said at last and, to Timothy's horror, a huge tear formed in the snailman's eye and trickled slowly down his hard, granite face.

The friendship between Timothy and Bob Mimms seemed to infuriate the Paynes, driving them to greater frenzies of torment. Day after day they would appear at the snailman's gate, chanting their childish rhyme, "Bad old Bob. He's a slob . . . ," and Timothy, hearing them, would blush and bite his lips in embarrassment. But the snailman appeared not to hear, and after a while Timothy did the same so that the silly voices became indistinct from the bleating of the sheep or the twittering of birds in the eaves. Even Crabby stopped growling when he heard them.

The dog had everything to content his canine heart now, a master to feed and house him and a small boy to romp with in the fields or scuffle with in mock fights on the mat in front of the fire.

At school the physical violence had stopped. It was as if Timothy Eden walked in the protective shadow of a giant of a man and the other children, sensing it, left him alone. But they hated him all the more. And, because they were too afraid to kick and punch him as they used to, they stepped up the only other form of torment they knew . . . a barrage of insults and vulgarities, which they hurled at the silent boy at every opportunity.

"Phew!" complained Harry Payne, grasping his nose and checking with a quick glance that he had everyone's attention. "What a 'orrible stink under me nose." And he jabbed a finger at Timothy's back. "It's those dirty ol' snails. Ugh! He really whiffs o' them."

"Ain't got no friends of 'is own," jeered Fatty Simons, "so 'e 'as to spend all 'is time with a crazy man."

"They're both crazy."

"Ought ter be in the funny farm, both o' them."

Timothy ignored the comments. It was difficult and sometimes he longed to shout back or punch the stupid bovine faces, but he knew his contemptuous silence was a far greater insult to them. He knew because the snailman had told him so, and there was nobody in the world he believed more than the snailman.

And then Timothy's world fell apart. He came home one day to be greeted by a very irate mother.

"I thought I told you not to visit that man," she raged.

"What man, Mum?" Timothy was all innocence.

"Don't be smart with me," she advanced on him, wagging a finger. "You know precisely who I mean . . . that awful Bob Mimms."

"But he's not awful, Mum." Timothy was stung to the quick. What did his mother know of the snailman? She had never seen him, never spoken to him. "He's really a nice . . . ," he began, but was abruptly silenced.

"Don't go near him again, do you understand? If I hear

57

you've even set foot in his house, I'll . . ."

But he never heard what punishment was in store for him because he ran from the room, out into the garden, and up into the horse chestnut tree, where he could hide, protected by a canopy of thick green leaves.

His mind was in turmoil. Never to see the snailman again was unthinkable. His mother had to be some kind of a monster to suggest it. Just because she was miserable, did she have to spoil the one good thing that had happened to him in Stourley?

After a while he heard her calling from the kitchen. "Timothy, it's supper time. Come and get washed, please."

He ignored her.

"Timothy, do you hear me? Timothy?" She was standing at the foot of the tree, peering up, trying to find her son among all the foliage. "Timothy, will you please come down or I shall get really angry. . ."

But Timothy didn't budge. There was nothing to come down for.

In the early evening, as the shadows were lengthening, his father appeared.

"Timothy, come down, there's a good chap."

Silence.

"You don't want to stay up there all night, do you? It will get very cold, you know, and you'll be starving by morning."

Silence.

He heard his father sigh. "I'm disappointed in you. I thought you were growing up."

58

An hour later, when the garden was in darkness and small animals rustled through the undergrowth, Timothy climbed down the tree, slowly because his legs were cramped and he was cold.

His father was sitting at the table, his head in his hands, but he got up quickly when Timothy came in.

"Do you want to talk about it now, old fellow?" he said, putting an arm around his son's shoulders.

Timothy shook his head, too choked for words.

Mrs. Eden looked as if she had been crying and Timothy knew from his father's flushed, angry face that there had been another argument between them. "This time, it's all because of me," Timothy said to himself, as he dragged himself up the stairs to bed. And he wished he were dead.

"Reckon as how your friend's got hisself in a bit of a pickle," said Mr. Thompson the next morning, looking over the fence into Timothy's garden. "Seems his dog has been worryin' Farmer Bideford's cows. . . ."

Timothy put a finger to his lips and pointed to the kitchen to indicate that his mother mustn't hear. Then he went out into the lane.

"What happened?" he said, his eyes wide with anxiety, as he and the old man walked towards Springett's pond.

"Well, Bob goes a-visitin' an old lady every Friday evenin', year in, year out, come rain or shine. Deaf she is, poor old Granny Forbes, so I don't know what they do, the pair o'

them, her as deaf as a post and him never saying nothin'
nohow." The old man chuckled. Timothy wished he'd get to
the point. "Any road, he always goes to see her, like I said,
six-thirty sharp every Friday, with some food in the basket,
tomatoes and cabbages and other things he grows hisself
. . . and a bottle of beer or two 'cos the old lady likes her
beer but she can't get to the local no more, not with her
arthritis, that bad it is. . . ."

Timothy sighed.

"She lives on the other side o' Tunney's pasture, so Bob
takes a shortcut through Bideford's fields," continued Mr.
Thompson, speeding up his story for the benefit of the im-
patient boy. "But it's a shortcut that's led him into a load of
trouble this time 'cos that there dog of his chases some of the
cows that were in calf. And now the calves are all born dead.
Hundreds of pounds old Bideford has lost. He's real sore about
it."

"But how do they know it was Crabby?"

"'Cos folks seen him and Bob, that's how."

Timothy was dejected. "What will happen?"

"Don't rightly know." The old man eased himself onto a
bench by the side of the pond and stretched his aching legs.
"I hear as how Bideford were in the Griffin last night, carryin'
on alarmin'. Says he'd been to see Bob Mimms but Bob denied
everythin'. Says his dog never chases anythin' . . . not even
rabbits, though I finds that hard to believe meself."

"It's true!"

"Any road, there's talk of Bideford getting his own back. Maybe he'll call in the local constabulary or do somethin' hisself. Though I don't know what."

But Timothy soon discovered what. The next day, despite his mother's warning, he stole up Carpenters' Hill and over the snailman's gate. The door to his house was closed. Timothy was puzzled—usually it was open and Bob was sitting weaving.

Timothy knocked but there was no answer. He knocked again, and then, very cautiously, he opened the door and peered round it.

The snailman was sitting by the fire, Crabby at his feet, gazing up at him sadly. Something was wrong with his master but the dog didn't know what and it whimpered and pawed at him.

"Hullo," said Timothy, feeling it was a very ineffectual greeting in the circumstances.

The man turned, looked at him and, without a word, pointed to the corner of the room.

Timothy turned to look and his heart missed a beat. The beautiful loom was broken, smashed to pieces, its frame beyond repair.

He picked up the shuttle, the only part that had escaped destruction, and held it in his hand, looking helplessly at the snailman.

"It were me mother's loom," said the snailman, in a toneless voice. "She taught me to use it."

Timothy didn't know what to say. He felt grieved for the

snailman, because he knew how dear the loom was to him, but words like "I'm sorry" or "What a pity" weren't enough to express the sadness he felt.

And he wondered how Bob would earn a living now that his precious loom was gone.

"How did it happen?" he whispered finally.

"I hears a noise in the back field, somebody shouting, 'Help! Help!' so I runs out with Crabby, but when I gets there, there's nobody around. So I comes back in and . . ." He indicated the broken loom.

"You mean somebody came in here and deliberately smashed it?" Timothy was shocked to the very center of his being. People just didn't behave like that. He sat down heavily opposite the snailman, his mind confused by the violent turn of events.

"Was it . . . could it have been Farmer Bideford?" he said at length, hesitating to accuse somebody because of hearsay.

The snailman shrugged. "Bideford thinks old Crabby was the reason his cows lost their calves."

"Tell the police," said Timothy hotly.

"Ain't got no proof it were him."

Timothy had seen enough police dramas on television to know that proof was important in a court of law. And, in any case, Farmer Bideford had good reason to be angry.

"It wasn't Crabby, was it?" he cried, grabbing the snailman's arm impetuously.

"Crabby ain't no cattle worrier. You know that well as I do."

Timothy hung his head, ashamed. Of course he knew that. Bob Mimms and Crabby were the gentlest beings in the whole of Stourley.

There was an air of suppressed excitement in school the next morning. Everybody was talking about the destruction of the snailman's loom. Harry Payne swaggered and, whenever he caught Fatty Simon's eye, he winked broadly. Clearly he was beside himself with delight.

"Poor ol' Bob," he said in a loud voice, to nobody in particular. "'E's been and gone a bit too far this time, 'e 'as, letting 'is moth-eaten old mutt chase ol' Bideford's cows."

Timothy went red but said nothing, his eyes glued to a book.

"I do 'ear tell as 'ow Bideford is sayin' next time it 'appens, 'e'll put a bullet in that mutt's 'ead."

Timothy felt the muscles in the back of his neck stiffen with tension.

"An' if that don't stop it, 'e'll probably put a bullet in the snailman too. Course, that'll be no loss. I think 'e'd be better off dead anyway. Good riddance to bad rubbish. I mean . . ." but before Harry Payne could explain what he meant, Timothy was on him, pounding his head and chest with clenched fists, his face congested, contorted with fury.

Harry collapsed under the assault and, instead of helping, the other children gathered round, screaming with delight and urging them both to greater excesses.

"Stop it! This minute! Timothy, I hardly expected such a display from you!"

Timothy slunk back to his seat, unable to look at Miss Forfar. He had let her down . . . but it had been well worth it.

64

"The two of you will report to me after school," she said, slamming her books on the desk in a rare display of impatience. "I am really getting rather tired of the hooliganism in this class."

"You talk to him," said Mrs. Eden to her husband when Timothy finally got home late that afternoon. "Maybe you can do something with him, because I can't."

And she stomped off to her bedroom and slammed the door so that the whole house seemed to shake.

Timothy's father sighed and leaned back in his chair.

"You're certainly getting into some silly scrapes lately," he said, looking at his son in a despairing kind of way. "And you always used to be such a sensible kid."

He paused, waiting for Timothy to explain, but the boy was upset and confused. He had been plunged into a grown-up world of revenge and violence, of hatred and contempt, and it frightened him more than he cared to admit.

He was even more afraid of the feeling it aroused within himself. He wanted to kill anyone who tried to hurt the snailman or Crabby. . . .

"It just isn't fair!" he blurted out as an extension of his thoughts.

"What isn't fair? Oh, you mean this vendetta thing that's going on between Bideford and Bob Mimms, I suppose?"

Again he waited for some sort of response.

"Stay out of that scrap," he warned sternly. "It's not the kind of thing a ten-year-old would want to get mixed up with.

And for that matter, neither would I . . . and I'm four times your age. It's a dirty business . . . whatever the truth may be."

Timothy opened his mouth to speak but changed his mind. He had always been able to talk to his father, but lately the tension in the house, his mother's unhappiness, his own loneliness, and the relentless persecution of the village children had somehow come between them so that they faced each other now in a stiff, formal fashion.

The realization that he was losing his father sank Timothy even deeper into the pit.

"You've been seeing a lot of this man Mimms," continued Mr. Eden. "He must be something special."

Timothy contemplated his knees.

"Well?"

"He's nice."

"That's a bit weak, Timothy." His father began to sound irritated. "There are plenty of 'nice' people around, and closer to your own age, too."

"Not around here," mumbled Timothy.

Mr. Eden leaned forward and spoke to him in an earnest voice. "Look, I know it's a drag for you living in Stourley, but if you'll hang on for a year, just one year, you'll be going to a new school, a much bigger one than this little tin pot affair in the village, and everything will be different. You'll make plenty of friends there and you'll only come back here for the holidays."

The thought depressed Timothy even more. A school full of Harry Paynes and Fatty Simonses from morning to night was nothing to look forward to.

Mr. Eden looked at his son's dejected face and he sighed, a deep, racking sigh that came from the depths of his heart. He passed a hand wearily across his forehead in an effort to wipe away the problems that seemed to be pressing in on him.

"I wish now I'd stayed in London," he said, so quietly Timothy could hardly hear him. "I thought I was doing the right thing, the best thing for all of us. . . ." His voice faded away and he sat, gazing into space, a sad expression on his face.

Timothy fidgeted nervously.

"Look," said his father finally, "I don't know much about Bob Mimms. I've seen him once or twice and he doesn't look very savory to me. I know that doesn't mean anything," he added, as Timothy glowered, "but he's a funny kind of guy from what I've heard. A bit antisocial . . ."

"You should meet him," muttered Timothy, interrupting his father. "Why don't you come up to his house with me and you could . . . well, you could talk."

A small doubt filtered into his mind. The snailman was the last man on earth to engage in social chitchat. But his father dismissed the suggestion with a wave of his hand.

"I will, old fellow. I promise," he said. "One day. But not just now. Let the whole thing drop, will you? For your mother's sake. She's a bit overwrought at the moment."

Unwillingly, unhappily, Timothy agreed.

That evening, in the privacy of his bedroom, Timothy wrote a letter. It took a long time and he tore up so many sheets of his mother's special writing paper there was hardly any left in the box by the time he had finished. He had wondered how to address it.

"Dear Bob," he wrote. No, that was disrespectful. And he never called him Bob anyway.

"Dear Mr. Mimms." Too formal. Timothy doubted that the snailman had ever been called Mr. Mimms in his whole life.

Finally he settled on "Dear Mr. Snailman and Crabby, My mother says I am not to see you again because I have to find friends of my own age. I'm sorry about this but hope you will understand. Your affectionate friend, Timothy.

"P.S. I miss Crabby.

"P.P.S. I miss you."

He put the letter in an envelope and sealed it. Too late he remembered something else he should have said. He toyed with the idea of steaming the envelope open again, then changed his mind and, picking up his pen, he wrote on the back, "P.P.P.S. I miss Ted and Jake too."

He slipped out of the house, while his mother and father were in the back garden pruning the fruit trees, and ran like the wind up Carpenters' Hill. As he drew near the snailman's house he slowed down and crept along the hedgerow until he was only a few yards from the old tin mailbox with "Bob Mimms" painted on its side.

He dreaded lest the snailman should come out and see him. He would have to give him the letter and see the hurt expression on the man's face when he read it.

For a long moment, Timothy agonized, looking up and down the lane desperately for some kind of help. Finally he lunged forward and rammed the letter in the mailbox. The lid fell back with a clang and Timothy turned tail and ran back as fast as he could.

As he closed the front door behind him, he heard an old, familiar, detestable refrain. It was the Payne boys, stomping past the house, on their way to their favorite evening's entertainment.

"Bad old Bob. He's a slob.

"No one wants to give him a job," they caroled at the tops of their voices for Timothy's benefit.

"So he has to cadge and rob.

"Bad old, sad old, mad old Bob."

Timothy watched them go, their faces flushed with pleasure.

"Bad old, sad old, mad old Bob!" wafted back down the hill, the voices growing fainter and fainter.

"Bad old, sad old, mad . . ."

They were off to persecute the snailman again, to jeer and taunt, and throw stones at Crabby. And there was nothing Timothy could do. Nothing. Burying his head in his hands, he wept.

Something was happening at school, something Timothy couldn't understand and wasn't allowed to share. Children gathered in tight little knots and chattered, their eyes shining with mischievous pleasure. Harry Payne strutted around as if he were King Tut, and he and Fatty Simons seemed to be always together, joking and nudging each other, especially when Timothy was nearby. The excitement mounted during the week until, by Friday afternoon, it had reached fever pitch. On his way home from school, Timothy had a burning desire to see the snailman, to warn him . . . of what? He didn't know.

He hung around outside the gate on Carpenters' Hill, hoping the snailman would see him and come out to talk. He fancied it would not be breaking a promise if the snailman came to him. But the house was silent and nobody apppeared.

Finally, in despair, Timothy hit on a notion. Searching in his schoolbag for a scrap of paper, he wrote on it, "I think something nasty's going to happen. Please be careful," and, wrapping it round a stone, he threw it as hard as he could against the door.

The warning sounded ineffectual. What was the something that was going to happen? He didn't know. How should the snailman be careful? He couldn't say. If only he could have spoken with the man face-to-face, he could have told him of the electricity in the air, the tension, the mounting excitement that builds up to a major thunderstorm.

Seconds passed before the door opened. Crabby saw the boy first and came bounding toward the gate, yelping with delight. The snailman looked puzzled. Timothy pointed frantically at the stone and, as the man bent to pick it up, he ran off down the hill, leaving a very disappointed dog gazing at his retreating back in utter bewilderment.

It didn't work. The snailman ignored his advice and went across the Bideford property, stubbornly, determinedly, visiting Granny Forbes the way he always had every Friday night since his parents had died. And again a dog was seen chasing cattle.

"Another four calves found dead this mornin', all stillborn," said Mr. Thompson as he and Timothy sat in the old man's kitchen the following day. "It's a bad business. A bad business," and he sucked his teeth noisily to express his concern.

"Who saw Cr— I mean, who saw the dog that did it, Mr. Thompson?"

"Roland and Betsy Jones. They was on their way to the Griffin for a pint or two on Friday evenin'. They see Bob Mimms and his dog crossin' the field and . . ."

"Did they actually see Crabby chasing cows?" persisted Timothy.

"Not actually sees him," said Mr. Thompson, frowning a little. "But he were there . . . and so were the cows . . . so it stands to reason he did it, don't it?"

Timothy couldn't see any logic in that.

"Perhaps there was another dog."

"Oh, well, nobody's heard tell of it if there were."

Another dog. The thought grew in Timothy's head. Was Crabby being blamed for another dog's mischief? Was Crabby being deliberately vilified, so that his master would suffer?

Who would play such a dirty game? And why?

Timothy tossed it back and forth in his mind the whole weekend. He wanted to go and see the snailman, to talk to him, but he had made a promise to his father and he couldn't break it.

He was still thinking about it on Monday morning as he walked into school for yet another dreary week.

The atmosphere was electric. The class waited silently, almost breathlessy, for him to appear.

"'Eard the latest?" demanded Harry Payne, as Timothy threw his satchel on the desk and sat down.

Timothy spun around but the boy was gazing at a spot on the ceiling, a look of sweet innocence on his round, vacuous face.

The other children giggled and nudged each other. They had a smug, "We know something you don't know" look on their faces that irritated Timothy.

"What is the latest?" retorted Fatty Simons, trying not to laugh.

"'Bout poor ol' Bob Mimms."

"Do tell."

"'E ain't a snailman no more."

The class exploded into guffaws.

"Seems some 'orrible person 'as killed all 'is lovely snails . . . smashed 'em to a pulp. Ain't that a wicked thing to do, eh?" And he collapsed into hysterical giggles.

Timothy felt the room swim. It wasn't true. It couldn't be true. It was just Harry Payne's sick sense of humor.

They were waiting for him to say something. But he disappointed them. He wasn't going to let Harry Payne or Fatty Simons or any of them get a reaction out of him.

He sat tight until the first break and then, when he was sure nobody had noticed, he slipped out of the gate and ran down Carpenters' Hill. He didn't care about playing truant from school. He didn't care about breaking the promise to his father. He just had to see the snailman. Nothing else mattered.

It was true.

All the snails were dead, their shells crushed, their bodies unrecognizable. The snailman had left them as he found them that morning, their battered bodies strewn across the shelf and floor of the shed. Not one had been spared.

Timothy was numb. He stood for a long while, staring at the desolate scene in the shed, then he went into the cottage.

The snailman was sitting in his usual chair, his hands resting on the sides, his head back, as if he were asleep. But he turned as the boy came in and stared mutely at him.

Timothy opened his mouth to speak, but no words came. He wanted to say something that would comfort the man, but his mouth was dry and the words stuck in his throat.

He put a hand on the snailman's arm and then ran from the cottage. He wanted to run away, a long way from the horror that threatened to engulf him. But he couldn't leave the snail-man all alone. Not now. So he dragged himself back into the shed and slowly, methodically, like a mechanical man, he collected what remained of the pathetic snails and carried them to the far end of Bob Mimms's property. There, while Crabby watched, he dug a hole and, piling the snails in a box, which he had lined with tissue paper, he placed them in their grave and gently patted earth on top. On a piece of paper he wrote, "For Jake and Ted and all my friends," nailed it to a stick, and pushed the stick into the soft earth.

Crabby whined uneasily and pawed at the little grave. But Timothy didn't cry. His chest heaved in silent sobs, but no sound came from him and no tears touched his cheeks.

He stared at the stick for a long time, reading and rereading the inscription, "For Jake and Ted and all my friends," until the words swam before his eyes.

Then he slowly turned and walked away.

Mrs. Bideford answered the door. When she saw the boy standing there, her face blossomed into a big smile.

"It's Timothy Eden, isn't it? Come on in. . . ." She hesitated. "But shouldn't you be at school?"

Timothy gazed at her blankly.

"What's wrong?" she said, putting an arm around his shoulders and bending down until her face almost touched his.

"I'd like to see Mr. Bideford," said Timothy in a small, strangled voice.

"Well of course, dear." She looked momentarily flustered. "He's out in the yard with his foreman just now, but he'll be in shortly. Is there anything I can do?"

Timothy shook his head, his jaw clenched.

"Come into the kitchen with me. You look that upset," she said. "I'll get you a nice mug of hot chocolate and maybe a piece of home-made gingerbread. Would you like that?"

She pushed the boy ahead of her into a big, bright room, its walls lined with copper kettles and pans.

"Sit there, m'dear," she said, indicating a place at the trestle table that seemed to stretch from one end of the kitchen to the other.

Timothy drank the chocolate and ate the cake like a robot, his arm rising and falling automatically, his big dark eyes staring straight ahead. Mrs. Bideford was making bread, her rough, reddened hands kneading a great ball of dough on a floury board. She chattered all the while, occasionally glancing at the small, silent boy.

At last, to her obvious relief, Mr. Bideford came in. He was a tall, heavily built man with a mop of red hair, and he looked very surprised when he saw Timothy.

"You've got company, I see, Mother," he said to his wife, laughing. But she shook her head quickly to indicate the matter was serious.

"It's Timothy . . . the Edens' boy."

Mr. Bideford frowned.

"The new people on Orchard Lane, next to the Thompsons," she explained.

"Oh, yes, of course. Hullo, Timothy."

"He's come to see *you*."

They both stood and looked at the boy, Mr. Bideford puzzled, his wife wringing her hands on her apron in a nervous gesture.

Timothy slid off the stool. He didn't know what he was going to say. He only knew he was sick at heart.

"Mr. Bideford"—he looked the farmer right in the eye—"why did you kill all Bob Mimms' snails? Couldn't you have left him one? Jake or Ted or . . ." but the great lump in his throat choked him.

He wasn't going to cry, he told himself sternly, pressing his lips together to stop them from trembling. He wasn't going to cry . . . not in front of this man. Mr. Bideford sat down heavily. His wife started to say something, but he raised his hand to silence her.

"Leave us for a while, would you, Mother?" he said. And she went out, closing the door softly behind her.

"Sit down, Timothy."

He had a strong, no-nonsense voice.

"Do I look like a mean, vindictive person?"

They stared at each other.

"Do I look like the kind of person who would destroy a man's livelihood and kill something he loved?"

Timothy swallowed hard.

"I don't like the things that are going on in Stourley any more than you do," continued Mr. Bideford. "And I don't like to see my cows lose their calves, either. I take good care of them all through the winter, feed them, shelter them, buy a champion bull to service them, and then . . ." His voice hardened. "Some fool of a mutt chases them all over God's half-acre and they drop their calves before time." He paused, pulling a pipe out of his pocket and ramming tobacco into it in an agitated kind of way. "But I don't lay blame where there's no proof," he said, "and I certainly don't take the law into my own hands. If Bob Mimms is guilty . . ."

"But he isn't!" Timothy blurted out. "Crabby wouldn't do that. He's a good dog."

Mr. Bideford nodded, sucking on his pipe thoughtfully. "We'll see about that," he said. "We'll see."

On Friday afternoon it began to rain, a gentle drizzle that soon increased to a downpour. Timothy looked anxiously at the water streaming down the windows.

"Timothy!" Miss Forfar's voice cut sharply across his thoughts. "I said, can you give us a definition of a mammal?"

"A mammal?"

It was quiz time again. Timothy tried desperately to get his mind back into focus.

"No, I'm sorry, I can't," he said sheepishly.

Miss Forfrar sighed. Her star pupil was letting her down badly. She opened her mouth to say something caustic and abruptly changed her mind.

"You nig nog," whispered Harry Payne, leaning forward so that Timothy could hear. "You ain't so bright after all," and he jabbed a pen into Timothy's neck.

Timothy clenched his jaw and stared at the blackboard. Out of the corner of his eye he could see Fatty Simons gloating.

"Hey, Timothy." It was Harry Payne again. "Seen any dead snails lately?" and he chuckled, as if it were a huge joke.

It was still raining at a quarter to four, and Timothy ran down Carpenters' hill, water dripping down his neck and squelching in his shoes. As he drew near his home, he slowed down and began to drag his steps.

"Hullo, sweetheart," his mother greeted him at the door with a smile. "You look like a damp squib," she laughed, helping him off with his coat.

Timothy stared at her over his shoulder. He hadn't heard his mother laugh, not really laugh, since they left London.

Delicious smells wafted from the kitchen.

"I've made a special treat." His mother pushed him ahead of her. "Go and see."

A huge chocolate cake was cooling on a wire rack. Timothy's eyes lit up.

"Want a piece while it's still warm?" she said. As he ate, his mother sat and watched him.

"Would you mind if Daddy and I went out this evening?" she said, after a while.

Timothy's heart leaped. He had made great plans for the evening, plans he did not want his parents to know about. All day he had worried how he could get them both out of the house, just for a few hours, without their suspecting anything. And now his mother had solved the problem for him. It was too good to be true.

"It's just a little celebration," she went on. "You see, I've got a job at last." She laughed at Timothy's astonished face. "I'm going to be Dr. Laurie's receptionist. He has a very busy practice and I'll have lots to do. . . ."

So that was why she looked so happy.

"We'll get a sitter, of course. I'm sure Mrs. Paget's daughter will come over . . . you like her, don't you?"

Timothy's expression registered indignation. "I don't need a sitter, Mum. I'll be eleven in October! You can leave me alone. I'll be good, promise I will."

Mrs. Eden looked doubtful and shook her head.

"What if there's an emergency?"

"I'll go next door to Mr. Thompson. He's a nice old man. He'd help."

"What do you think, Roger?" said his mother when Mr. Eden came home.

"Oh, he'll be all right," said Mr. Eden, ruffling Timothy's hair. "And we'll be back by nine . . . nine-thirty at the very latest. Nothing much can go wrong in a couple hours."

"Did you reserve a table at the Binnacle?"

Her husband nodded. "For half past six."

Timothy bit his lip in frustration. Half past six was too late.

"Oughtn't you to leave now?" he suggested.

His mother burst out laughing. "Now? But it's only a quarter to six. We'd be there in fifteen minutes." She pulled him toward her. "I believe you want to get rid of us."

"No. No!" Timothy's protest was too vehement, and his mother frowned.

"What's wrong?"

80

"Nothing. I . . . I just want you to enjoy yourself." It sounded feeble, and Mrs. Eden wasn't convinced. "May I go out and play?" he asked, trying to avoid her questioning eyes.

"No, I want you to eat your supper and do your homework, and after that you may watch television for an hour."

It seemed to Timothy that it took an eternity for his parents to dress for dinner, but at last, at long last, they were gone. He waved furiously until their car was out of sight and then he pulled on a coat and scarf, rammed a cap over his eyes and shot out of the front door, slamming it behind him. A horrible thought struck him too late. He had no key to get back in.

"Oh, well," he shrugged, "I'll worry about that later," and, pausing only to glance at his watch, he vaulted the garden gate and ran down Orchard Lane as fast as he could.

He arrived at Bideford's pasture just after six thirty. Checking to see that nobody was watching, he climbed over the gate into the field and ran along the hedgerow for a hundred yards or so. From this vantage point he could see the stile at the foot of Carpenters' Hill and the path that led from it to the gate at the other end of the field.

Timothy crouched low and backed into a hedge. It was still wet with raindrops and water trickled miserably down the back of his neck. He pulled his scarf up until it was under his chin, rammed his hands in his pockets and lay still, watching the stile, waiting for the familiar figure of Bob Mimms.

The minutes crept by and, though Timothy stared till his eyes smarted, nobody appeared.

Seven o'clock. His heart sank. Maybe the snailman wasn't coming after all. Maybe tonight of all nights, the snailman wasn't going to visit Granny Forbes.

Timothy felt like crying with frustration. All week he had planned this. All week he had racked his brain to find a way of getting out of the house for a few hours . . . and his mother had given him a heaven-sent opportunity. And now . . . The field was empty, quite empty.

He stretched his legs. The ground was horribly wet and drops kept splashing on him. He shivered and called himself all the fools for not having thought to bring a blanket or groundsheet. To make it worse, he couldn't even go home. He had locked himself out.

All the excitement had gone. Suddenly Timothy felt silly, all his grandiose plans for exonerating Crabby and restoring the snailman to a place of honor in the eyes of the community seemed useless and futile.

"Timothy Eden, supersleuth," he said to himself scathingly. Only kids on television were supersleuths . . . and that was all fantasy and make-believe anyway.

A movement at the end of the field caught his eye. He squinted hard. Could it be . . . could it possibly be . . .? Of course it was the snailman. He recognized the slow, lurching gait. And there was dear old Crabby, gamboling about like a puppy, running ahead and stopping to wait for his master. But not once, not for one second, did he go anywhere near Farmer Bideford's cows, Timothy noticed.

"Good boy, Crabby," he breathed. "Good dog."

It was a quarter past seven. Bob had been to see Granny Forbes and was on his way home again. Slowly he crossed the field, with Crabby staying fairly close to his heels. When they reached the stile, the dog flattened himself out and slithered underneath, the man hauling himself awkwardly over the top, and they disappeared from view.

"Now," thought Timothy, a small pulse in his neck beginning to beat with excitement. "Now what?"

The shadows were lengthening. The day was coming to an end. Timothy watched the sun disappear slowly, slowly behind the hills until the world was plunged into darkness.

A noise in the bushes nearby made him jump. With every nerve strained, he squinted into the shadows. "What a fool I am not to have brought a flashlight," he scolded himself . . . and started violently as a rabbit hopped out of the hedge and disappeared into the night.

Timothy could see the dark outline of cows in the deepening gloom. One was so close he could hear the scrunch, scrunch of her teeth as she chewed the cud. He began to feel uneasy. The familiar countryside was foreboding at night. Trees took on ominous shapes; the hoot of an owl, the screech of a bat became evil sounds, like something out of a nightmare.

The moon came out from behind a cloud and bathed the field in a pool of eerie light. Timothy peered at his watch. Nine o'clock already! His heart sank. His mother and father would be home any moment. What would they do when they

found his room empty, his bed not slept in? Should he leave
now, try to get home before them, make some silly excuse for
having been out? He shook his head in answer to his own
questions. He had to wait it out. He had to.

An hour passed. His legs were stiff with cold but still he
dared not move or make a sound. The rustlings around him
increased. All the animals were on the move now, stoat after
rabbit, owl after mouse, fox after . . . Timothy sat bolt up-

right. Something, some fairly large animal, had detached itself from the shadows and was bounding into the field. An excited barking broke out, followed by the distressed lowing of cows.

Timothy could have jumped for joy. It was a dog, *the* dog, and it was after Farmer Bideford's cows again!

Stiffly, stumbling awkwardly, he got to his feet. He had to catch that dog; he had to catch it and drag it to the police station so that Crabby's name would be cleared.

He stepped out into the field, squinting into the darkness. From the sound of it, the dog was somewhere to his right. He ran forward, calling and whistling. "Here, boy! Here!"

"'Ere!" rapped a voice so close to Timothy's ear he nearly died of fright. "What d'you think you're up to, eh?"

Timothy wheeled and saw a man running at him out of the darkness, his arms outstretched, menacing.

Timothy shrieked and started to run away, but after a few yards his left foot disappeared down a rabbit hole and he fell flat on his face. The next moment a shaft of light streaked across the field.

"Stay where you are!" boomed a voice. "Both of you!"

Timothy lay still, his heart pounding so hard it was almost beating its way out of his rib cage. A flashlight was turned full on his face.

"I know him," said a vaguely familiar voice. "It's young Timothy Eden. It's not him you want. It's this wretch." And the light was turned on to the man who had chased Timothy across the field.

The boy gasped. "Hey," he said, recognizing the sly, insolent face but not the name that went with it, "it's . . . it's . . ."

"Rennet Miller," the familiar voice obligingly added, and Timothy suddenly realized it was Farmer Bideford speaking. "And you can call off that dog of yours, Rennet," he added, almost spitting the words into the man's downcast face. "It's caused quite enough trouble these past few weeks, though you'll pay for it . . . and handsomely."

"But why . . . ?" Timothy began, thoroughly confused by now. He had been quite sure it was one of Fatty Simons's mangy curs, aided and abetted by Harry Payne. But Rennet Miller . . . ?

"I hired this man just after Christmas," explained Farmer Bideford, ignoring Rennet as if he were a lump of earth. "He was a poor worker, a lazy wretch who was more often asleep in the hay than cleaning out the barn. Lots of things went wrong while he was on my payroll. Eggs and cream disappeared, money was stolen, and some of my best men, chaps who had been at the farm for years, suddenly turned sour against me. For no reason. At least, I thought there was no reason. Then I began to discover the truth. This—" and he pointed at Rennet Miller, who scowled back, his thin, dry lips twisted in a contemptuous sneer. "So I fired him. But Rennet's a sore loser. He didn't like losing a cushy job, and when he slunk away, I knew I was in for trouble."

"You mean, it's his dog that's been worrying your cows?"

"His dog!" It was Mr. Bideford's turn to sneer. "He's never owned a thing in his life. He probably found the poor devil and keeps it half starved so it will be vicious."

"Oh shurrup!" snarled Rennet Miller, spitting on the ground to show his contempt. "You make me sick!"

The policeman who had been holding the torch took Rennet's arm in a viselike grip and frogmarched him back to a police car waiting in the lane.

Timothy sighed. Maybe the long, cold wait in the hedgerow had chilled his brain, but he still didn't understand.

"But who broke the snailman's loom, Mr. Bideford, and"—
he could hardly bring himself to say it—"and who killed all
his snails?"

"One and the same person," said the farmer curtly. "Rennet
Miller. He planned it so that it would look as if Bob Mimms's
dog was doing all the damage, then smashed the loom and
the snails to make it look as if I were taking revenge on poor
old Mimms. It's the work of a nasty, sick little mind,
Timothy."

"But why did he pick on the snailman, Mr. Bideford?"
Timothy was still confused. "The snailman's never done any
harm to Rennet Miller. . . ." And then he stopped short, for
he suddenly remembered that Rennet had suffered a sound
thrashing at the hands of the snailman.

The wretched tramp had tried to take revenge on both
Farmer Bideford and the snailman by playing one off against
the other.

Timothy's face went white with anger. "I'll . . . I'll
. . ." A thousand hideous tortures went through the boy's
mind, but none seemed harsh enough for Rennet Miller.

The farmer laid a hand on his shoulder. "Don't worry," he
said reassuringly. "Rennet will get the punishment he deserves
. . . a good, long spell behind bars where he can't hurt anyone.
But"—he paused and looked at the boy intently—"I still don't
understand what you are doing here at this time of night."

So Timothy explained, and when he got to the part where
his parents had gone out for the evening, leaving him, as they
thought, safely at home, Mr. Bideford looked grim.

"Timothy, I'd better get you home," he said. "It's almost eleven o'clock."

Timothy's heart sank. Now he was really for it. "Let's hurry," he urged Farmer Bideford, and the two of them set off at a run.

Timothy's parents had already called the police and were beside themselves with worry but somehow, in some miraculous way, the farmer managed to persuade them that what their son had done was not so terrible after all. In fact, to Timothy's amazement, Mr. Bideford made him out to be something of a hero, a "champion of the underdog," as he kept saying.

"I wish there were more kids like him," he concluded, looking at Timothy in such a way that the boy flushed with embarrassment and hung his head.

"As long as you're safe, darling," said his mother, drawing him into her arms and holding him very tightly, "that's all that matters."

"Mum," said Timothy, snuggling closer to her. "Do you think I could be . . . friends with the snailman again?"

Her body stiffened.

"Oh, please," he pleaded, looking to Farmer Bideford and his father for support. "He's such a nice man. Really he is. You'd like him. . . ."

"All right. All right," Mrs. Eden conceded, exchanging a look with her husband.

"Come on, old man," said Mr. Eden briskly. "A bath to warm you up, a mug of hot chocolate, and into bed with you."

And, throwing Timothy over his shoulder, he stomped upstairs with him.

Timothy was about to protest that he was too old to be carried up the stairs in a fireman's lift but he changed his mind. After all, his mother was smiling, his father was laughing and—though he wouldn't have admitted it for the world—he secretly enjoyed being babied. Now and again.

The next morning he woke when it was still dark, and, slipping out of bed, he dressed quickly and quietly. The stairs creaked loudly and Timothy's heart stopped . . . but no sound came from his parents' bedroom.

He had left a note pinned to his pillow so as not to give his mother another nasty shock. It said, quite simply, "Have gone to pick mushrooms. Back soon."

The sun was just beginning to peer over the hills as he closed the front door behind him. The air felt good, as cool and crisp as an icicle. Timothy smiled, pleased with himself and happier than he had been for a long time. He had the snailman for a friend again. His mother had agreed to that. And he had a new friend, Mr. Bideford, who had invited him over to the farm any time he cared to call.

He would go over that very day, Timothy thought, have some of Mrs. Bideford's good gingerbread and take a ride on one of the huge farm horses. But, in the meantime, there was work to be done and, buttoning up his coat to keep out the early morning chill, he set off determinedly for Tunney's pasture.

Once there, he crouched down on hands and knees and started searching. Oh, how he searched. He turned over every stick and stone and leaf from one end of the field to the other until his legs ached, his back screamed, and his sleeves were soaked with dew.

The sun came up higher and higher and still Timothy couldn't find what he was looking for.

He became desperate, moving along the hedgerow, turning over rocks and kicking aside leaves in a frenzy. And then, at last, his search was over.

Beaming like a Cheshire cat, his heart lighter than a lark's, he put his find in a paper bag and set off at a brisk trot up Carpenters' Hill.

The door of the snailman's house was open and Crabby was sitting on the step, surveying his property with a very lordly air. His immediate reaction to the sight of Timothy scrambling over the gate was to growl, but when he recognized his old friend he bounded to greet him, overwhelming him with licks and welcoming nips on the ear.

The snailman was in the kitchen, cooking breakfast. He looked up sharply as Timothy came in.

"I'm allowed," said the boy quickly. "Mum says it's all right. Did you hear about Rennet Miller?" he burst out excitedly. "It was his dog that worried Farmer Bideford's cows."

"So I do hear from ol' Mr. Thompson," said the snailman.
He pointed to the frying pan, where eggs and bacon sputtered
in the hot fat. "Breakfast?"

Timothy nodded. He was famished. "I hope they put Rennet
in prison for life," he said, his eyes lighting up at the thought
of the many tortures he hoped the unfortunate man would
have to undergo. "I hope they thrash him and . . ."

"Don't say that," said the snailman quietly. "Rennet's to
be pitied more'n punished."

Timothy bit his lip. He ought to have known the snailman
would say that.

"I have something for you," he said shyly, holding out the brown paper bag he had carried so carefully from Tunney's pasture.

The snailman put down the fork he was holding and looked at the bag suspiciously.

"What is it?" he demanded.

"A present." Timothy thrust the bag at him. "It's for you. Please take it."

The snailman gave a grunt of disbelief. "Don't usually get no presents," he said doubtfully. But he took the bag, opened it, and drew out the biggest snail that ever was. Its huge shell rested in the palm of his hand and, as Timothy watched, it slowly appeared, stretching out its head and weaving great tentacles from side to side in a questioning motion.

The snailman had a strange expression on his face, but he said nothing. Not even "Thank you."

"We can start another snail colony," said Timothy, who was quite used to the man's lack of conventional manners. "This one's a beauty, isn't he? Isn't he? I searched all over Tunney's pasture for him. I found thousands of snails," he babbled excitedly, "but not one that could hold a candle to him. He must be at least five inches long and look at the size of his shell . . . it's . . . it's almost as big as my fist, isn't it? What shall we call him? Hey, let's call him Jake . . . no, Ted. Yes, we'll call him Ted, okay?"

Despite himself, Timothy was a little disappointed that the man showed no emotion . . . no pleasure, no excitement, no gratitude. Nothing. Perhaps, thought the boy, some of his own pleasure abating, perhaps it had been wrong to bring him a snail as a gift . . . even a snail as big as this one. Perhaps it had revived painful memories that brought sorrow rather than the happiness Timothy had hoped for.

He began to feel uncomfortable.

At last the snailman looked up, and placing a hand on Timothy's shoulder, he looked at him intently.

"It's my present, my snail, ain't it?" he demanded gruffly.

Timothy nodded.

"Then I can name it meself?"

"Yes, of course."

"Reckon I'll name it after someone I know, then," said the snailman. "A good friend o' mine. The best friend I ever had." And he smiled for the first time. "Reckon I'll call it Timothy."

About the Author

After living and traveling in France and Africa for a few years, Brenda Sivers settled in Montreal for several years. She has now returned to her native England, where she has bought an old coachhouse in the heart of the English countryside. In spite of a demanding professional life as journalist, magazine editor, and, at present, public relations officer, Ms. Sivers continues to work at her avocation, writing for children. *The Snailman* is the recipient of the Little, Brown Canadian Children's Book Award.